THE BOY WHO BROUGHT
THE SNOW

For Samuel, Nathan and Charlotte — *H.H.*

For Ella, Benji, Sierra and Amelie — *A.W.*

BLOOMSBURY CHILDREN'S BOOKS
Bloomsbury Publishing Plc
50 Bedford Square, London WC1B 3DP, UK
29 Earlsfort Terrace, Dublin 2, Ireland

BLOOMSBURY, BLOOMSBURY CHILDREN'S BOOKS and the Diana logo are trademarks of Bloomsbury Publishing Plc

First published in Great Britain in 2023 by Bloomsbury Publishing Plc

A catalogue record for this book is available from the British Library

ISBN HB: 978 1 5266 0966 3
ISBN PB: 978 1 5266 0965 6
ISBN eBook: 978 1 5266 0967 0

1 3 5 7 9 10 8 6 4 2

Printed in China by Leo Paper Products, Heshan, Guangdong

To find out more about our authors and books visit www.bloomsbury.com and sign up for our newsletters

THE BOY WHO BROUGHT THE SNOW

written by

Hollie Hughes

illustrated by

Anna Wilson

BLOOMSBURY
CHILDREN'S BOOKS
LONDON OXFORD NEW YORK NEW DELHI SYDNEY

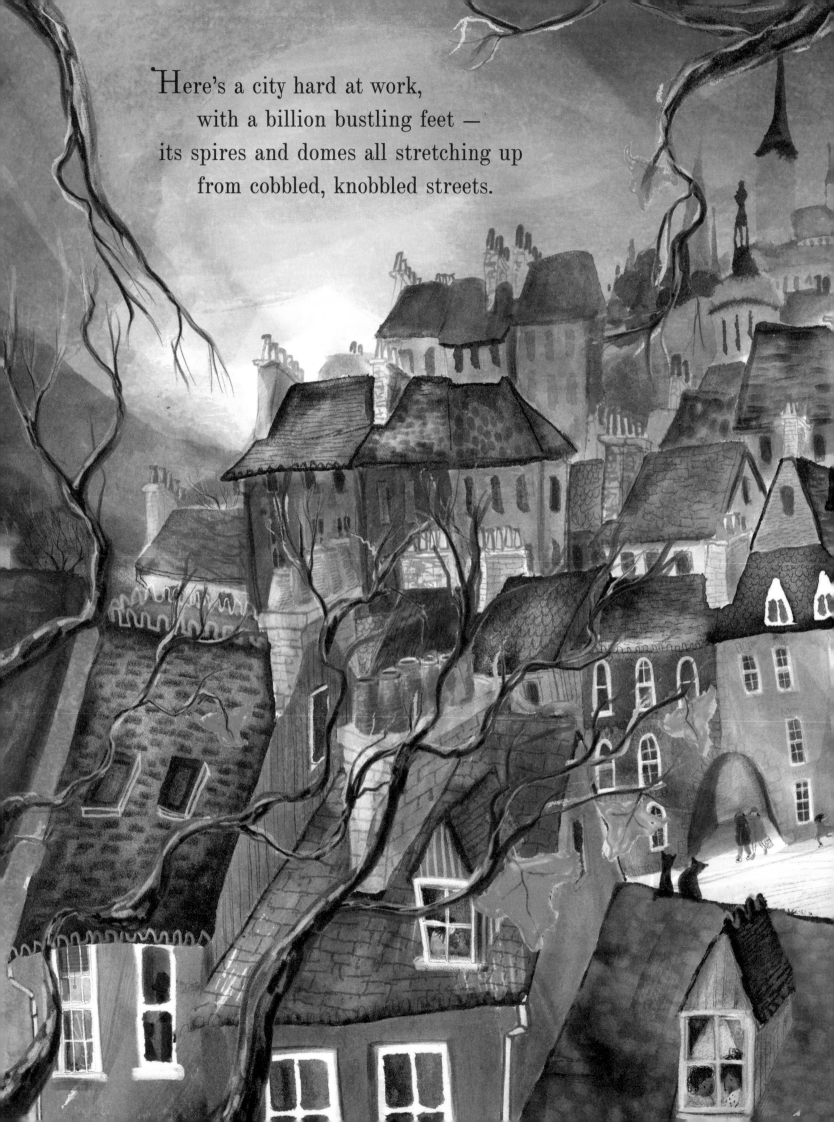

Here's a city hard at work,
  with a billion bustling feet —
its spires and domes all stretching up
  from cobbled, knobbled streets.

And here's a bench in the middle,
   where Quinn sleeps every night,
together with his mum and dad —
   they're hidden in plain sight.

The busy feet walk past them,
    not one person sees them there.
The city has forgotten
    to remember how to care.

But, late one night, Quinn stirs to find
a magic glowing dome.
A snow globe of the city,
and the folk who call it home.

In the centre of the globe,
    rests a bench just like his own.
And, on the bench, a boy like him —
    a child without a home.

He gently gives the globe a shake,
    and snow begins to fall,
drifting down to settle
    on the city in the ball.

In the morning Quinn is woken,
and is dazzled by the sight
of a city blanketed by snow
that's fallen in the night.

There's a robin perched beside him,
with a chirp to say hello,
and Quinn sees that the city
looks quite different in the snow . . .

For the freeze has
slowed the city down,
reminding folk to care.

They are helping others out now,
and remembering to share.

They are shovelling paths
through snow drifts,
and delivering milk and bread.

There is time not just to talk,
but to listen now instead.

And there's also time for play,
and a snow day in the park . . .

on sledges made from pallets,

slipping,

sliding . . .

into dark!

That night Quinn grips the snow globe,
and he gently shakes it up.
"Please work again," he wishes,
crossing everything for luck.

And it does send snow the next day . . .

and then many after too!

And, with his robin friend,
Quinn finds more
snowy things to do.

The more Quinn shakes the snow globe,
        the more it keeps on snowing.
And the deeper that snow drifts,
        the more kindness keeps on growing.

It seems to Quinn so perfect
        he can't ever let it end,
or go back to his life before
        the snow brought him a friend.

But the city starts to long for warmth
and, in his heart somehow,
Quinn knows the time for spring is here,
and winter must stop now.

Though he worries, without snow,
things will never be the same,
he sets the globe aside, and sighs —

he won't make it snow again.

In the shining morning light, Quinn sees
that spring has come at last,
and the city's bustling back to work,
just like in days gone past.

But, as the hours and minutes fly,
each moment seems to show
that folk are helping out still —

even though there is
no snow!

Yet there's something special
missing — that flash of
brightest red.

The robin of the snow is gone,
and worries crowd Quinn's head.

Quinn searches everywhere he can,
with ever-deeper dread.

But, still, he cannot find
his friend, and now
it's time for bed.

But benches are not beds for boys,
in cities that can care,

and here — at last! — the robin comes,
to gently lead Quinn where . . .

There's a budding garden hedge,
with a twig for birds to rest,
and, snuggled just behind, he finds
a warm and cosy nest!

And, while beaks have carried twigs
to build that nest for hungry chicks . . .

Hands that learnt to share again have shifted wood and bricks.

Friends that shovelled pavements, and delivered food to eat,
have been busy building up from love . . .

a new house on the street.

So, here in this great city,
    amidst shining spires and domes,
    for Mum, and Dad, and Quinn, at last
        is a warm and cosy . . .